W9-AFR-711

GATEWAY TO

# MYSTERY

## STORIES

*Illustrated Short Story Classics*

Elayne Sidley, Editor

Sherman

Published by Target Press, Carson, California

Distributed by Oak Tree Publications, San Diego, California

136699

**The Gateway to Mystery Stories is part of the Gateway series.**

*The Gateway to Mystery Stories* copyright © 1978 by Target Press.

First Edition
Manufactured in the United States of America
Distributed by Oak Tree Publications, Inc.
For information write to: Oak Tree Publications, Inc.,
P.O. Box 1012, La Jolla, CA 92038.

Library of Congress Cataloging in Publication Data
Main entry under title:

Gateway to mystery stories.

(The Gateway series)
CONTENTS: Doyle, C. The adventure of the speckled band.--Henry, O. After twenty years.--Chekov, A. The bet. [etc.]
1. Detective and mystery stories. [1. Mystery and detective stories. 2. Short stories] I. Sidley, Elayne.
PZ5.G3163 [Fic] 78-5487
ISBN 0-916392-20-1

# CONTENTS

The illustrations for this book are by Alice Abramowitz, Douglas Bruce Berry, Mike Hodgson, Ernie Kollar, Louis Maytorena, Darryle Purcell, Don Rico, and Wendell Washer.

ACKNOWLEDGMENTS

Grateful acknowledgment is made to the following for permission to adapt and reprint published material:

*Mystery at the Library of Congress* copyright © 1960 by Ellery Queen. Reprinted by permission of the author and the author's agents, Scott Meredith Literary Agency, Inc., 845 Third Avenue, New York, New York 10022

# THE ADVENTURE OF THE SPECKLED BAND

*by Sir Arthur Conan Doyle*

Sherlock Holmes

Dr. John Watson

Helen Stoner

Dr. Grimesby Roylott

Like myself, Sherlock Holmes was a late riser. It was much to my surprise one morning when he woke me very early to tell me we had a visitor. I dressed quickly and we went into the sitting room together. A young lady, veiled and dressed in black, was sitting by the window.

"Good morning, madam," said my friend. "My name is Sherlock Holmes. This is my friend and associate, Dr. Watson. Please draw near the fire, for I see that you are shivering."

"It is not the cold," she answered. "I am so frightened, Mr. Holmes." She raised her veil and we could see by her face that this was true.

"You must not be afraid," Holmes said quietly. "We shall soon put things right. You came by train this morning, I see."

"You know me, then?"

"No, but I can see the return ticket in the palm of your left glove. You started early, yet you had a drive in a dog-cart, along muddy roads, before you reached the station."

The lady jumped up and stared at my friend.

"There is no mystery," said he, smiling. "The left arm of your jacket is splattered with mud. Only a dog-cart throws up mud in that way."

"You are quite right," said she. "I started from home before six. Sir, I can stand this strain no longer; I shall go mad if it continues. The horror of it lies in the fact that my fears are so vague."

"I am all attention, madam."

"My name is Helen Stoner. I live with my stepfather, Dr. Grimesby Roylott, at Stoke Moran manor house. My mother met and married my stepfather in India. She was then a young widow. My twin sister Julia and I were just two years old. Shortly after our return to England, my mother was killed in a railway accident. Dr. Roylott took us to live with him at Stoke Moran.

"A terrible change came over our stepfather about this time. He shut himself up in his house, coming out only to quarrel with the neighbors. He is a man of great strength and uncontrollable anger. His only friends are the gypsies whom he allows to camp on his land. He also has a passion for Indian animals. He keeps a cheetah and a baboon, which move freely about the grounds.

"My poor sister died just two years ago. She had met a man to whom she became engaged. But two weeks before the day of the wedding, a terrible thing happened."

"Please be precise as to the details," said Holmes.

"Only one wing of the house is now occupied. The bedrooms are all on the ground floor. The first bedroom is Dr. Roylott's, the second my sister's, and the third my own. They all open out into the same corridor.

"The fatal night Dr. Roylott had gone to his room early. Julia was troubled by the smell of his cigars, and she came into my room. We talked till about eleven. As she left, she asked me if I ever heard anyone whistle in the dead of night.

" 'Never,' said I. 'But why?'

" 'Because the last few nights I have been awakened by a low whistle. I cannot tell where it comes from. Well, it is no great matter.' She returned to her room, and I heard her lock her door.

"It was a wild night and I could not sleep. The wind was howling and the rain beating against the window. Suddenly I heard a horrible scream. As I rushed into the corridor, I heard a low whistle such as my sister had described. Then there was a clanging sound, like a falling mass of metal.

"My sister was standing in the corridor, swaying, her face white with terror. As I ran to her she fell, shaking, as if in terrible pain. 'Oh, Helen!' she shrieked. 'It was the band! The speckled band!' My stepfather came hurrying from his room, but by then Julia was unconscious. She died in spite of all efforts to revive her.

"The coroner was unable to find a cause of death. It seemed impossible that the room could have been entered, with the door locked and the window shutters barred."

"How about poison?"

"The doctors examined her for it, but without success.

"A month ago, a dear friend asked my hand in marriage. Shortly after that, some repairs were begun on the house. I have had to move into my sister's room, sleeping in her bed. You can imagine my terror when suddenly, late last night, I heard the low whistle again! As soon as it was daylight I started out to see you."

"You have done wisely," said Holmes. "Would it be possible for us to come to Stoke Moran today? And could we see these rooms without the knowledge of your stepfather?"

"Yes; he was coming to London today on business."

"Good! Expect us then this afternoon."

After breakfast Holmes left the house. He returned at one o'clock with a sheet of figures in his hand. "I have been studying the late Mrs. Roylott's will," he said. "The doctor would lose most of his money if both girls married. The marriage of even one of them would impoverish him to a great extent."

9

Suddenly the door was dashed open, and a huge man filled the doorway.

"Which of you is Holmes?" he asked.

"My name, sir, but you have the advantage of me," said my friend quietly.

"I am Dr. Grimesby Roylott."

"Indeed, Doctor," said Holmes blandly. "Pray take a seat."

"I will do nothing of the kind. My stepdaughter has been here. I have traced her." He took a step forward. "I have heard of you! You are Holmes, the busybody. Don't you dare to meddle in my affairs. I am a dangerous man to fall foul of. See here!" He seized the fireplace poker and bent it with his huge brown hands.

"See that you keep out of my grip," he snarled, and hurling the twisted poker into the fireplace he strode out of the room.

"He seems a friendly sort," said Holmes, laughing. "Had he remained, I might have shown him that my grip is not much weaker than his own." He picked up the steel poker, and, with a sudden effort, straightened it again.

Helen Stoner was waiting for us when we arrived at Stoke Moran that afternoon. Holmes looked first at the plainly furnished room that she was now occupying. He made sure that the barred shutters could not possibly be opened from the outside. Then he turned his attention to a ventilator above the bed, and the bell rope just above it.

"Why, it's a dummy!" he said, giving a tug at the thick rope. "It's just fastened to a hook."

"I never noticed that," said Miss Stoner. "It was put there just two years ago, at the same time as the ventilator."

"Yes, I see. A ventilator that opens into another room, rather than to the outside air."

So saying, Holmes led us into the doctor's room next door. It was also plainly furnished. Its most noticeable feature was a large iron safe.

"What's this?" said Holmes. He was looking at a dog whip, hanging by the bed. Its end was tied into a loop.

"Miss Stoner," he said, "you must absolutely follow my advice. Your life may depend on it. First, Watson and I must spend the night in your room. Stay there until your stepfather goes to his room. Then open your shutters. Put your lamp there as a signal. After that, go quietly into the room you used to occupy."

Miss Stoner willingly agreed, and Holmes and I made our way to the inn. We took a room facing the manor house.

"This is a bad business, Watson," said Holmes, as we sat in the gathering darkness. "I would advise you to bring your gun tonight."

"Really, Holmes!" said I. "You have seen more in these rooms than was visible to me."

"No, but I fancy that I may have deduced a little more. Dummy bell ropes and ventilators that do not ventilate."

"But the opening is so small that a rat could hardly pass through."

"I knew we would find a ventilator in that room."

"My dear Holmes!"

"Oh, but I did! You remember that Miss Stoner said her sister could smell Dr. Roylott's cigars! And did you notice that the bed was clamped to the floor? It could not be moved away from the bell rope and the ventilator."

"Holmes," I said, "I think I see what you are hinting at. We may be only just in time to prevent a horrible crime!"

"Horrible enough. When a doctor turns wrong, he is the worst of criminals."

At the stroke of eleven a bright light shone from Miss Stoner's window. We made our way silently across the grounds. We were about to enter the window when out of the bushes darted what seemed to be a hideous, deformed child. It threw itself onto the grass, then ran swiftly off into the darkness.

Holmes' hand closed like a vise upon my wrist. Then he broke into a low laugh. "It is a nice household," he said. "That is the baboon."

I remembered that there was a cheetah as well. I confess I breathed more easily when I found myself inside Miss Stoner's room.

Holmes quietly closed the window and removed the lamp. "We must sit without a light," he whispered. "He could see it through the ventilator."

We waited in the dark. The village clock struck midnight, one, two, three.

Suddenly there was a momentary gleam of light from the ventilator. There followed a soft hissing sound. Holmes sprang up instantly. He struck a match and lashed furiously with his cane at the bell rope.

"You see it, Watson?" he cried. "You see it?"

I could see nothing. Holmes had stopped lashing and was staring at the ventilator. Then the silence was broken by a horrible scream.

"It is all over," said Holmes. He lit the lamp. "Take your gun, and we will enter Dr. Roylott's room."

Dr. Roylott sat on a wooden chair, the dog whip on his lap. His eyes were fixed in a dreadful, rigid stare. Around his head was bound a strange yellow band with brownish spots.

"The band! The speckled band!" whispered Holmes.

The strange headgear began to move. From Roylott's hair rose the squat, diamond-shaped head of a snake.

"It is a swamp adder," said Holmes. "The deadliest snake in India. Roylott has died within seconds of being bitten." Holmes drew the dog whip from the dead man's lap. He slipped the noose around the snake's head, and, carrying it at arm's length, threw it into the open safe and clanged the door shut.

The next morning we took Miss Stoner to the care of her aunt at Harrow. On the train Holmes told me all that I had yet to learn about the case.

"At first," he said, "I thought 'the speckled band' referred to the gypsies, and the spotted handkerchiefs they wear around their heads. But after examining the door and the windows, I realized that nobody could have come through either. Then upon seeing Miss Stoner's bedroom, I suspected that the bell rope must be a bridge for something passing through the ventilator to the bed. I immediately thought of a snake, especially considering the doctor's Indian pets. The poison would not be detectable by any known chemical test. The whistle, of course, was to recall the snake. The metallic clanging Miss Stoner heard was the door of the safe being closed upon its occupant.

"When I heard it hiss last night, I attacked it, driving it back through the ventilator. I had aroused its snakish temper, and it flew upon the first person it saw. In this way I am indirectly responsible for Dr. Roylott's death. I cannot say that it weighs heavily on my conscience." □

# AFTER TWENTY YEARS

*by O. Henry*

The policeman moved up the avenue impressively. The impressiveness was habitual and not for show, for there were few people around. The neighborhood kept early hours. Most of the doors belonged to business places that had long since closed.

About midway in a certain block the policeman suddenly slowed his walk. In a darkened doorway a man leaned, with an unlighted cigar in his mouth. As the policeman came near, the man spoke quickly.

"It's all right, officer," he said. "I'm just waiting for a friend. It's an appointment made twenty years ago. Sounds a little funny, doesn't it? Well, about that long ago there used to be a restaurant here."

" 'Big Joe' Brady's," said the policeman. "It was torn down five years ago."

The man in the doorway struck a match and lit his cigar. "Twenty years ago tonight," he said, "I dined here with Jimmy Wells, my best chum and the finest chap in the world. We were raised here in New York together, just like brothers. Well, we agreed that night that we would meet here in exactly twenty years, no matter what our conditions might be or how far we might have to come. The next morning I started west to make my fortune."

"It sounds pretty interesting," said the policeman. "Haven't you heard from your friend since then?"

"Well, yes, for a time we corresponded," said the other. "Then after a year or two we lost track of each other. But I know Jimmy will meet me here if he's alive. He'll never forget."

The waiting man pulled out a handsome watch, the lids of it set with small diamonds.

"Three minutes to ten," he announced. "It was exactly ten o'clock when we parted twenty years ago."

"Did pretty well out west, didn't you?" asked the policeman.

"You bet! I hope Jimmy has done half as well. He was kind of a plodder, though, good fellow as he was. I've had to compete with some of the sharpest wits going to make my pile."

The policeman twirled his club. "I'll be on my way. Hope your friend comes around all right. Going to call time on him sharp?"

"I should say not!" said the other. "I'll give him half an hour at least. If Jimmy is alive on earth he'll be here. So long, officer."

"Good night, sir," said the policeman, passing on along his beat.

There was now a fine, cold drizzle falling, and the wind had risen into a steady blow. In the doorway the man smoked his cigar and waited.

About twenty minutes later a tall man in a long overcoat, with collar turned up to his ears, hurried across from the opposite side of the street. "Is that you, Bob?" he asked doubtfully.

"Is that you, Jimmy Wells?" cried the man in the door.

"Bless my heart," exclaimed the new arrival, grasping both the other's hands with his own. "It's Bob, sure as fate. Well, well, well—twenty years is a long time. How has the West treated you, old man?"

"Bully; it's given me everything I wanted. You've changed lots, Jimmy. I never thought you were so tall."

"Oh, I grew a bit after I was twenty."

"Doing well in New York, Jimmy?"

"Moderately. I have a job with the city. Come on, Bob, let's go to a place I know of, and have a good long talk about old times."

The two men started up the street, arm in arm. At the corner stood a drugstore, brilliant with electric lights. When they came into this glare, each man turned to gaze upon the other's face.

The man from the West stopped suddenly and released his arm. "You're not Jimmy Wells," he snapped. "Twenty years is a long time, but not long enough to change a Roman nose into a pug."

"It sometimes changes a good man into a bad one," said the tall man. "You're under arrest, 'Silky' Bob. Chicago wired us that you may have dropped over our way. Going quietly, are you? That's sensible. Now, before we go to the station, here's a note I was asked to hand you. You may read it here at the window. It's from Patrolman Wells."

The man's hand was steady when he began to read, but it trembled a little by the time he had finished. The note was rather short.

> *Bob:*
> *I was at the place on time. When you struck the match to light your cigar, I saw it was the face of the man wanted in Chicago. Somehow I couldn't do it myself, so I got a plainclothesman to do the job.*
> *Jimmy*

# THE BET

## by Anton Chekov

It was a dark autumn night. The old banker was pacing about his study, remembering the party he had given fifteen years before. There had been many people there, and they had been talking of capital punishment. Most of the guests said executions were immoral, and thought they should be abolished.

"I don't agree," said the host. "Execution kills instantly, life imprisonment kills by degrees. Which, then, is more cruel?"

Among the company was a lawyer, a man of about twenty-five. "They are both equally cruel," he said, "but if it were my choice, I would certainly choose life imprisonment. It's at least preferable to death."

"It's a lie," the banker cried out. "I bet you two million you couldn't remain in a cell even five years."

"If you mean it," said the lawyer, "then I bet I can last fifteen."

"Fifteen?" cried the banker. "Done!"

"Agreed! Your money against my freedom!"

And so this wild bet had come to pass. The banker, who had more money than he could count, was certain that the lawyer could not last more than three or four years.

The thought that at any moment he could free himself would prove too much for him.

It was agreed that the lawyer would be imprisoned in the garden wing of the banker's own house. He could have no contact with people, not even letters or newspapers. He was allowed to have a musical instrument, to read books, to write, even to drink wine if he wished. All of these he could receive by sending a note through the window. But he was obliged to remain in solitary confinement for exactly fifteen years.

At first he seemed to suffer terribly from loneliness and boredom. He played the piano day and night. He read popular novels: love stories, comedies, crime, and fantasy.

In the second year the piano was silent and the lawyer read only classics. In the fifth year music was heard again and the prisoner asked for wine. All during that year he did nothing but eat, drink, and lie on his bed. At night he would sometimes sit and write for hours, then tear it all up in the morning. Often he was heard weeping.

In the sixth year the prisoner began to study languages, philosophy, and history. He fell upon these subjects with such hunger that the banker hardly had time to get enough books for him. After the tenth year he sat motionless at his table and read only the Bible. This was later replaced by the history of religions and theology.

During the last two years, the prisoner read without pattern; now science, now Shakespeare. He read as though he were swimming in the sea, grasping one piece of wreckage after another in a desire to save his life.

At last, the fifteen years were done. "Tomorrow at midnight he goes free," the banker thought. "It will be all over with me. . . . " The banker was now ridden with debt. Gambling on the stock market had brought his business to ruin. Paying the lawyer would ruin him completely.

"That cursed bet," the old man murmured. "He's only forty years old. He will take my last penny and enjoy life while I look on like a beggar. No, it's too much. There's only one escape for me—the man must die!"

The clock had just struck three. Everyone in the house was asleep. Soundlessly, the banker took from his safe the key to the door that had not been opened in fifteen years. He put on his overcoat and left the house. Outside it was dark and cold. The wind whined through the frozen trees.

Approaching the garden wing, the banker called aloud for the watchman. There was no answer. Evidently he had fallen asleep.

"Good!" he thought. "If I kill him, the suspicion will fall on the watchman."

The old man peeped into the little window. The prisoner sat by the table, his back to the window. A candle was burning dimly. Open books were strewn across the room. The banker tapped on the window, but the prisoner made no movement.

Cautiously, the banker put the key into the lock. It gave a rusty groan, and the door creaked open.

Before the table sat a skeleton of a man, yellow-faced, with a graying, shaggy beard. No one looking at him could have believed that he was only forty years old. On the table lay a sheet of paper on which something was written.

"Poor devil," thought the banker. "No doubt he's dreaming about money. He's already half dead. All I have to do is throw him on the bed and smother him with a pillow. No one will suspect anything. But first let us read what he has written here."

The banker took the sheet from the table and read:

"Tomorrow night, I shall be free. But before I see the sun again, I must declare before God that I despise everything men call the blessings of the world.

"For fifteen years I have done nothing but study earthly things. In your books I drank sweet wine, sang songs, loved beautiful women. In your books I climbed mountains, worked miracles, preached new religions, conquered whole countries. . . .

"Your books gave me wisdom. I have come to see that everything you value is empty, false, hopeless. Though you be proud and wise and beautiful, death will wipe you from the face of the earth.

"That I may show you my contempt for that by which you live, I reject the money which I once saw as paradise. I despise it now. Tomorrow I shall come out of here before midnight, and thus lose the bet."

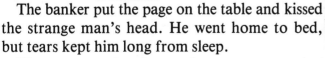

The banker put the page on the table and kissed the strange man's head. He went home to bed, but tears kept him long from sleep.

The next morning the watchman came running to him and told him that the lawyer had climbed out through the window and disappeared. The banker went immediately to the wing and confirmed that this was true. To avoid rumors, he took the sheet of paper from the table and locked it in his safe. □

# The Traveler's Story of a Terribly Strange Bed

*by Wilkie Collins*

Shortly after I finished college, I happened to be staying in Paris with an English friend. We were young men then, and lived rather a wild life in that delightful city. One night we were wondering what to do for amusement. "Let's go somewhere where we can see a little genuine, poverty-sticken gaming, with no false glitter thrown over it." "Very well," said my friend. "Here's just the place on this street."

When we got upstairs we were shown into the chief gambling room. I went to the table and began to play. I won incredibly. I won at such a rate that the regular players crowded around me. They stared at my stakes with hungry eyes, and whispered to one another that the English stranger was going to break the bank.

The game was *Rouge et Noir.* I had played it in every city in Europe. I never was a gambler in the strict sense of the word, but I had gone to gambling tables because they amused me, and because I had nothing better to do with my free time.

But on this occasion it was very different. Now, for the first time, I felt what the passion for play really was. My success first bewildered, and then, intoxicated me. I could do nothing wrong.

I bet higher and higher, and still won. The excitement in the room rose to fever pitch. Only one man in the room preserved his self-possession. That man was my friend. He begged me to leave, and be happy with what I had won. He left only after I had rejected his advice several times. I was, in a sense, gambling drunk.

Shortly after my friend had gone, a hoarse voice behind me cried, "Wonderful luck, sir! I give you my word of honor, I *never* saw such luck!"

I turned around and saw, nodding and smiling at me, a tall man, dressed in a decorated military coat. If I had been in my senses, I would have thought him a rather suspicious specimen of an old soldier. He had goggling, bloodshot eyes, a mangy mustache, and a broken nose. He had the dirtiest pair of hands I had ever seen—even in France. But in my mad excitement, I was willing to see anyone as a friend. "Go on and win! Break the bank," he said.

And I *did* go on, at such a rate that in another quarter of an hour, the *croupier* said, "Gentlemen, the bank has closed for tonight."

"Tie up the money in your handkerchief, my worthy sir," said the old soldier. "Your winnings will never fit in your pockets. And now, let us drink a bottle of champagne, and toast the goddess Fortune in foaming goblets before we part."

By the time the second bottle was emptied, I felt as if I had been drinking liquid fire. "Let us have a third bottle to put the flame out!" I cried.

The old soldier wagged his head and rolled his goggle-eyes. He said "Coffee!" and ran off into an inner room.

This word seemed to have a magical effect on the rest of the company. They all left at once. When the old soldier returned, we had the room to ourselves.

"Listen, my dear sir," he said, in mysteriously confidential tones. "Take my advice. You must drink this coffee. You are known to be a winner of an enormous amount by several gentlemen present tonight. Although they are excellent men, they have their weaknesses. Take a carriage home, and travel only on well-lighted streets. Do this, and your money will be safe."

Just then the coffee came in, poured out in two cups. I was parched with thirst, and drank it at once. Almost instantly I became giddy, and felt more intoxicated than before. The room whirled around furiously. I felt so dreadfully unwell that I did not know how I was to get home.

"My dear friend," said the soldier, "it would be madness to go home in *your* state. You might be robbed and murdered with the greatest ease. Sleep off the effects of the wine, and go home safely with your winnings tomorrow, in broad daylight."

I agreed to stay, and I was led up a flight of stairs into the bedroom which I was to occupy. After I was left alone, I washed my face in cold water, then sat down in a chair. My first thought was of the risk of sleeping all night in a gambling house; my second, of the still greater risk of going home alone at night through the streets of Paris with a large sum of money. I had slept in worse places than this on my travels, so I decided to lock, bolt, and barricade the door, and take my chance until the next morning.

I soon felt not only that I could not go to sleep, but that I was wide awake, and in a high fever. Every nerve in my body trembled. I tossed and rolled, and tried every kind of position. Every effort was in vain. I groaned, as I felt that I was in for a sleepless night.

What could I do? I had nothing to read. I remembered having once read a little book in which the author took an inventory of every piece of furniture in his room, and I decided to do the same.

There was, first, the bed I was lying in—a fourpost bed with a fringed canopy overhead. There was also a picture of a fellow in a high Spanish hat, crowned with a plume of feathers. My thoughts began to wander. I was thinking of past scenes and past amusements, when, in an instant, I found myself looking at the picture again.

Looking for what? Good God! Where was the hat? I looked up. Was I mad? Was the canopy of the bed really moving down, sinking slowly, regularly, silently, horribly, right down upon me?

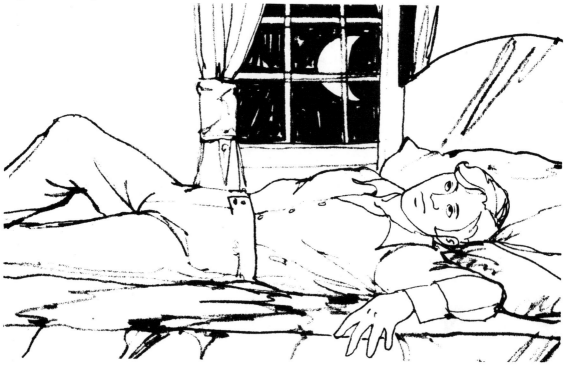

My blood seemed to stand still. A deadly, paralyzing coldness stole all over me. When I became convinced that the canopy was really moving, I looked up shuddering, helpless, panic-stricken. It was advancing closer and closer to suffocate me.

I was motionless, speechless, breathless. Down and down, without stopping and without sounding, came the canopy. Still my panic terror seemed to hold me to the mattress.

At the last possible moment the instinct of self-preservation startled me out of my trance, and I moved. There was just enough room for me to roll myself sideways off the bed. As I dropped noiselessly to the floor, the edge of the murderous canopy touched me on the shoulder.

I rose instantly on my knees to watch the canopy. It descended, so close that there was not any room to squeeze my finger between the canopy and the bed. I felt at the sides, and discovered that what had appeared to be a light canopy of a fourpost bed was really a thick, heavy mattress hidden by the fringe! In the middle of the canopy was a huge wooden screw that had evidently worked it down through a hole in the ceiling. There had been no creaking as it came down.

My cup of coffee had been drugged, and drugged too strongly. I had been saved from being smothered by having taken an overdose of some narcotic. How I had groaned at the fever fit which had saved my life by keeping me awake! How I had trusted the two wretches who had led me into this room, determined, for the sake of my winnings, to kill me in my sleep. How many men, winners like me, had slept in that bed, and had never been seen or heard of again?

About ten minutes passed. Then the canopy began to move up again. The bed looked like an ordinary bed again.

Now for the first time, I was able to move, to rise from my knees, and to consider how I should escape. If I made the slightest noise, I was certain to be murdered. Only one chance was left me—the window. It must have taken me at least five minutes, though it seemed like five hours, to open that window. I succeeded in doing it silently. Down the left side of the house ran a thick water pipe. It passed close by the outer edge of the window. The moment I saw the pipe, I knew I was saved. I had always been accustomed, by the practice of gymnastics, to keep up my schoolboy powers as a daring and expert climber.

I had already put one leg over the window sill, when I remembered the handkerchief filled with money under my pillow. I could well have afforded to leave it behind me, but I was determined that the villains of the gambling house should miss this plunder as well as their victim. So I went back to the bed and tied the heavy handkerchief to my back, using my necktie. The next moment I was again on the window sill—and the next I had a firm grip on the water pipe.

I slid down into the street easily and quietly, and immediately went to the police. When I had finished my breathless story, the officer put on his hat and ordered a file of soldiers to follow us to the house.

Guards were placed at the back and the front of the house the moment we got to it. A cry of "Open in the name of the law!" brought a waiter to the door. He, of course, denied that anything was wrong, but soon everyone in the house had his hands tied behind him. I identified the bed in which I had tried to sleep, and then we went into the room above.

The room looked quite ordinary, but the officer ordered the flooring to be carefully taken up. This was done in no time. We saw a deep cavity between the floor of this room and the ceiling of the room beneath. There was a case of iron thickly greased, and inside the case appeared the screw which attached to the canopy below.

We left the house later with two police agents in it. Every one of the inmates was removed to prison on the spot. I asked the officer, "Do you think that any men have really been smothered in that bed, as they tried to smother *me*?"

"I have seen dozens of drowned men laid out at the morgue, in whose pockets were found letters stating that they had committed suicide in the Seine, because they had lost everything at the gambling table. Do I know how many of those men entered the same gambling house that *you* entered? Won as *you* won? No man can say how many or how few have suffered the fate from which you have escaped."

The gambling house was searched carefully. Two of the less guilty made a confession. The "old soldier" was really the master of the gambling house. He had been drummed out of the army as a vagabond years ago. He, the *croupier*, another accomplice, and the woman who had made my cup of coffee, were all in on the secret of the bed. There was some reason to doubt that the other persons attached to the house knew anything of the bed. They received the benefit of that doubt and were treated simply as thieves and vagabonds. As for the old soldier and his two main followers, as well as the old woman who had drugged my coffee, they were imprisoned for I forget how many years.

One good result was produced by my adventure. The sight of a greencloth, with packs of cards and heaps of money on it, will always be associated in my mind with the sight of a bed canopy descending to suffocate me in the silence and darkness of the night. ☐

# THE LADY, OR THE TIGER?

### *by Frank R. Stockton*

A very long time ago, there lived a half-savage king. He was a man of wild fancy, and of such complete power that, at his command, he turned his fancy into facts. Whenever he and himself agreed on anything, it was done.

Among the ideas which he had borrowed from other kings was that of the public arena. But even here his fancy made itself known. The king's arena was used, not to give the people a chance to see dying gladiators, or the usual result of a contest between religious opinions and hungry beasts, but as a setting for poetic justice, through which the minds of his subjects were improved.

When a subject was accused of a crime, his trial would be held in the arena. When the seats were filled, the king would give a signal from his royal box. A door beneath him would open, and the accused would step forth. Directly opposite were two doors. They were side by side, and exactly alike. The accused would walk to one of these doors and open it. He could open either door he pleased. He was guided only by luck. If he opened the one, there came out a hungry tiger, which immediately tore him to pieces as punishment for his crime. Sad sounding iron bells were clanged, cries went up from hired mourners, and the crowd slowly made its way homeward, saddened that anyone should have deserved such a fate.

33

But if the accused person opened the other door, there came forth a lady, suitable to his years and station; and to her he was immediately married as a reward for his innocence. It mattered not that he might already have a wife. The king allowed no such arrangement to interfere with his justice. Gay brass bells rang forth merrily, the people cheered, and the innocent man, following behind the children who were throwing flowers in his path, led his bride home.

These trials were very popular. The people never knew whether they would be seeing a bloody killing or a joyous wedding. The perfect fairness was obvious. Did not the accused person have the matter in his own hands?

This half-savage king had a daughter, who was loved by him above all people. Among his subjects was a young man of that lowness of station usual among heroes of stories who love royal princesses. This princess was well satisfied with her lover, as he was handsome and brave to a degree above all others in the kingdom. This love affair moved on happily for many months. Then one day the king happened to learn of its existence. The king did not hesitate to do his duty. The youth was immediately thrown into prison. A date was set for his trial in the arena. This, of course, would be an especially important occasion. Never before had a subject dared to love the daughter of a king. The tiger cages of the kingdom were searched for the most savage beasts. The whole kingdom was searched for the most beautiful maiden.

The day arrived. From far and near the people gathered, packing the arena. Crowds of people unable to find seats massed themselves against the outside walls. The king and his court were in their places.

All was ready. The signal was given. A door beneath the royal party opened. The lover of the princess walked into the arena. His appearance was greeted by a low hum of admiration. Many in the audience had not known so grand a youth had lived among them. No wonder the princess loved him! What a terrible thing for him to be there!

The youth turned, as was the custom, to bow to the king. But his eyes were on the princess, who sat to the right of her father. From the moment it had been announced that her lover's fate would be decided in the arena, she had thought of nothing else. What was more, she had done what no other person had ever done—she had learned behind which door waited the tiger, and which the lady. Gold, and the power of her will, had brought her the secret.

In fact, she knew who the lady was. She was one of the fairest and loveliest maidens of the court. The princess hated her. Often she had seen, or imagined that she had seen, this fair creature looking at her lover. Now and then she had seen them talking together. It was but for a moment or two, but much can be said in a brief time.

When her lover looked at her, he saw by the power of quick understanding of those whose souls are one, that she knew the secret. He had expected her to know it. He understood what she was like. His hope in opening the right door was based on the princess learning the secret and giving him a signal. As he looked at her, he knew she had done so.

36

Her right arm lay on a cushion before her. She raised her hand and made a quick motion to the right. No one but her lover saw her. Every eye but his was fixed on the man in the arena.

He turned, and with a firm and rapid step he walked across the empty space. Every heart stopped beating; every breath was held. Without the slightest hesitation, he went to the door on the right, and opened it.

Now, the point of the story is this: Did the tiger come out of that door, or did the lady?

The more we think about this question, the harder it is to answer. Think of it, fair reader, not as if the choice rested with yourself, but with that half-savage princess. She had lost him, but who should have him?

How often had she covered her face in horror as she thought of her lover opening the door behind which waited the cruel fangs of the tiger!

But how much more often had she seen him at the other door! How she had gnashed her teeth and torn her hair when she saw his joy and delight! How she had burned when she saw him rushing to meet that woman! When she had seen him lead her forth! When she had seen them, man and wife, walk away together upon their path of flowers to the glad shouts of the crowd!

Would it not be better for him to die at once, and wait for her in the world of half-savage heaven?

And yet, that awful tiger, those screams, that blood!

Her choice had been shown in an instant, but it had been made after days and nights of painful thought. She had known she would be asked. She had decided what she would answer. Without the slightest hesitation she had moved her hand to the right.

The question of her decision is not to be lightly considered. It is not for me to dare to be the one person able to answer it. I leave it with all of you: Which came out of that opened door—the lady, or the tiger? □

# The Trial for Murder

## by Charles Dickens

I have always noticed that most people are reluctant to discuss strange psychological experiences. In what I am going to say, I do not want to set up, oppose, or support any theory whatever. I have not inherited any unusual powers, and I have never before had any similar experience, nor have I had such an experience since.

It does not matter when a certain murder was committed in England. I would like to bury the memory of this particular murderer, if I could, as his body was buried in Newgate Jail.

When the murder was first discovered, it was nowhere publicly hinted that any suspicion fell on the man who was later brought to trial. No reference was at that time made to him in the newspapers. So it is obviously impossible that any description of him was given in the newspapers. It is essential that this fact be remembered.

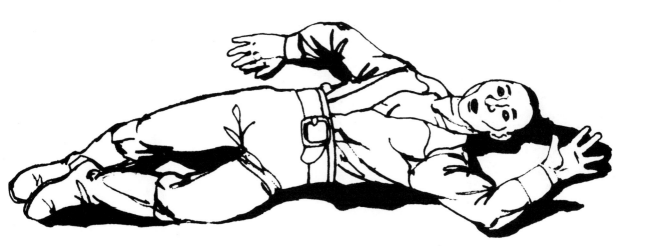

Reading my morning paper at breakfast, with the story of that first discovery, I found it to be deeply interesting. I read it with close attention. I read it twice, if not three times. The discovery of the murder had been made in a bedroom. When I laid down the paper, I was aware of a flash—rush—flow—I do not know what to call it—in which I seemed to see that bedroom passing through my room. It was like a picture impossibly painted on a running river. Though it passed almost instantly, it was perfectly clear.

When this happened I was at home in Piccadilly in a second floor room. I went to one of the windows. It was a bright autumn morning. As I watched the leaves being whirled around by the wind, I saw two men on the opposite side of the way. They were one behind the other. The one in front often looked back over his shoulder. The second man followed him, with his right hand menacingly raised. First, this threatening gesture in so public a place attracted my attention. Next, I was surprised that nobody noticed it. Both men moved with an unusual smoothness. No one, that I could see, touched them or looked at them. In passing before my windows, they both stared up at me. I saw their two faces very clearly, and I knew that I could recognize them anywhere. The man who went first had an unusually scowling appearance. The man who followed him was the color of impure wax.

A few nights later I was standing in my bedroom, giving some directions to my servant before he went to bed. My face was toward the door to the dressing room. The door was closed. My servant's back was toward that door. While I was speaking to him, I saw the door open. A man looked in, who very earnestly and mysteriously beckoned to me. That man was the man I had seen second of the two along Piccadilly—the one whose face was the color of impure wax.

The figure, having beckoned, drew back and closed the door. I immediately crossed the bedroom, opened the dressing room door, and looked in. I had a lighted candle already in my hand. I did not expect to see the figure in the dressing room, and I did not see it there.

Aware of my servant's amazement, I turned to him, and said: "Derrick, could you believe that I thought I saw a—" As I was speaking, I touched his arm. He suddenly trembled violently and said, "Oh Lord, yes, sir! A dead man beckoning!"

Now I do not believe that my servant was aware of having seen any such figure, until I had touched his arm. The change in him was so startling when I touched him, that I fully believe he got his impression in some strange manner from me at that moment.

The very next morning I received a call to serve on a jury. I decided, as a break in the dullness of my life, that I would go.

On a foggy and dark morning in the month of November, I took my seat in the place for jurors. Soon after, the judge entered and took his seat. The direction was given to bring in the prisoner. He appeared. In that same instant I recognized him as the first of the two men who had gone down Piccadilly.

As I stepped into the jury box, the prisoner saw me and became violently agitated. He beckoned to his attorney. *"Challenge that man!"* he demanded. But, as he would give no reason for it, it was not done.

I was chosen foreman of the jury. On the second morning of the trial, I looked over my fellow jurymen. I found a great difficulty in counting them. I counted several times, yet always found that there were thirteen of us.

I asked the juryman who was sitting next to me to count us. He looked surprised by the request, but turned his head and counted. "Why, we are thirt—. But no, it's not possible. No. We are twelve."

We were housed at the London Inn. We all slept in one large room, under the eye of the officer sworn to hold us in safekeeping. His name was Mr. Harker.

On the night following the second day, I didn't feel like lying down. I saw Mr. Harker sitting on his bed, so I went and sat beside him. I offered him a pinch of snuff. As Mr. Harker's hand touched mine in taking it from my box, a peculiar shiver crossed him, and he said, "Who is this?"

Following his eyes, I saw again the second of the two men who had gone down Piccadilly. As I rose, Mr. Harker said, "I thought for a moment we had a thirteenth juryman, without a bed. But I see it is the moonlight."

I didn't say anything to Mr. Harker, but I watched what the figure did. It stood for a few moments by the bedside of each of my eleven fellow jurymen. It seemed, from the action of the head, merely to look down thoughtfully at each sleeping figure. It took no notice of me, or of my bed. It seemed to go out where the moonlight came in, through a high window.

Next morning at breakfast, it appeared that everybody present had dreamed of the murdered man last night, except myself and Mr. Harker.

On the fifth day of the trial, a picture of the murdered man was put in evidence. As an officer in a black gown was getting ready to give it to me, the figure came from the crowd. He caught the picture from the officer, and gave it to me with his own hands, saying, *"I was younger then, and my face was not then drained of blood."* He then took the picture from each juryman to pass it to the next. Not one of them, however, detected this.

Until the fifth day of the trial, I had never seen the figure in court. But now that we had entered on the case for the defense, the figure was in court continually. In the opening speech for the defense, it was suggested that the deceased might have cut his own throat. The figure stood at the speaker's elbow, motioning across and across its throat, now with the right hand, now with the left, vigorously suggesting to the speaker himself the impossibility of such a wound having been self-inflicted by either hand. Another time, a witness to character tried to say that the prisoner was the most likable of men. The figure at that instant stood on the floor before her, looking her full in the face, and pointing out the prisoner's evil face with an extended arm and an outstretched finger.

45

It seemed as if the figure were prevented somehow from fully showing itself to others. Yet it could invisibly, quietly, and darkly influence their minds. For, although they could not see the figure, they were always somehow disturbed by it. When the idea of suicide was suggested, the lawyer faltered in his speech, wiped his forehead with his handkerchief, and turned pale. When the witness to character was confronted by the figure, her eyes most certainly did follow the direction of its pointed finger, and rested in great hesitation and trouble upon the prisoner's face.

The trial was finally over. We went out to consider our verdict. When we returned to the courtroom, the figure was standing directly opposite the jury-box, on the other side of the court. As I sat down, his eyes rested on me with great attention. He seemed satisfied, and slowly shook a great gray veil, which he carried on his arm for the first time, over his head and whole form. As I spoke our verdict, "Guilty," the veil collapsed, all was gone, and his place was empty.

The murderer was asked by the judge whether he had anything to say before sentence of death should be passed upon him. The declaration that he made was this: *"My Lord, I knew I was a doomed man when the foreman of my jury came into the box. I knew he would never let me off, because, before I was taken, he somehow got to my bedside in the night, woke me, and put a rope around my neck."* □

# THE GOLD-BUG

*by Edgar Allan Poe*

Many years ago I became friends with a Mr. William Legrand. He lived at Sullivan's Island, near Charleston, South Carolina. Not far from the eastern end of the island, Legrand had built himself a small hut, which is where he was living when I met him.

He had many books, but rarely used them. He loved gunning, fishing, and shell-collecting. He was usually accompanied by Jupiter, who had been freed from slavery by the family, but had stayed with Legrand.

Winters at Sullivan's Island were seldom very cold, and a fire is usually not needed. About the middle of October, 1840, however, it was very chilly. Just before sunset, I arrived at the hut of my friend. No one was home, so I looked for the key where I knew it was hidden, unlocked the door, and went in. A fine fire was blazing. I took off my overcoat, sat in an armchair by the fire, and waited patiently for the arrival of my hosts.

Soon after dark they arrived, and gave me a most cordial welcome. Legrand was very excited because he had found a beetle which he believed to be totally new. He could not show it to me right then, because he had given it to his friend Lieutenant George until the morning. "Stay here tonight," he said, "and I will send Jupiter down for it at sunrise. It is the loveliest thing in creation! It is of a brilliant gold color. The antennae are—"

Jupiter interrupted: "The bug is a gold-bug, solid, every bit of him, inside and all, except his wings—never felt half so heavy a bug in my life."

"You never saw a more brilliant luster," said Legrand. "But of this you cannot judge until tomorrow. In the meantime, I can give you some idea of the shape." Saying this, he seated himself at a small table, on which there were a pen and ink, but no paper. He looked for some in a drawer, but found none.

"Never mind," said he at length, "this will answer." He took what looked like a dirty scrap of paper from his vest pocket, and made a rough drawing with the pen. While he did this, I sat by the fire, for I was still chilly. As he handed it to me, there was a loud growl and a scratching at the door. Jupiter opened it, and let in a large Newfoundland, belonging to Legrand. The dog leaped upon my shoulders, and loaded me with caresses. When he finished, I looked at the paper, and was puzzled at what my friend had drawn.

"Well!" I said, "this *is* a strange beetle—
it looks like a skull, or a death's-head."

"A death's-head! Oh—yes—well, it has
something of that appearance on paper,
no doubt. The two upper black spots look
like eyes, and the longer one at the bottom
looks like a mouth—and then the whole
shape is oval."

"Perhaps so," said I; "but Legrand, I
fear you are no artist. Where are the
antennae you spoke of?"

"The antennae!" said Legrand. "I am sure you must see them."

He looked again at the paper, and was about to crumple it and throw it into the
fire, when a casual glance at it seemed suddenly to attract his attention. He
examined it carefully. Then he placed the paper in his desk, which he locked. The
rest of the evening he was very thoughtful and quiet, so I decided not to stay until
the morning as I had planned.

About a month later I received a visit from Jupiter. He told me that Legrand was very sick. Jupiter, in fact, thought that he had been bitten by the gold-bug, because he had been acting so strangely.

The letter Jupiter brought from Legrand was an urgent plea for me to come immediately. He said he had business of the *highest* importance.

Without a moment's hesitation I prepared to go with Jupiter. When we reached the boat, I noticed a scythe and three spades, all new, lying in the bottom of the boat. Jupiter explained that Legrand had insisted that Jupiter buy them in the town. "It's all because of that bug," said Jupiter.

We arrived at the hut about three in the afternoon. Legrand had been waiting for us eagerly. He was pale, and I began to think Jupiter was right about his health.

"Jupiter is right about that bug," he said. "It is a bug of *real gold*. This bug is to make my fortune. Is it any wonder that I prize it?"

He then showed me the bug. It was a beautiful beetle, and, at that time, unknown to naturalists—of course a great prize from a scientific point of view. The scales were hard and glossy, and looked like burnished gold. The weight of the insect was very remarkable. But it hardly seemed as important as Legrand and Jupiter thought.

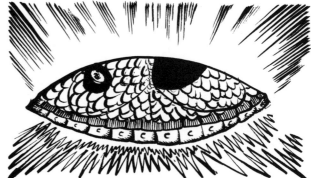

"My dear Legrand," I said, "you are not well. You shall go to bed, and I will remain with you a few days, until you get over this. You are feverish and—"

But he would hear nothing of this, and insisted that he was well. "Jupiter and I are going to the hills, upon the mainland, and we need help. You are the only one we can trust. We will start immediately, and be back by sunrise."

With a heavy heart, I went with my friend. We started about four o'clock—Legrand, Jupiter, the dog, and myself. Jupiter carried the scythe and spades, I carried a few lanterns, and Legrand carried the bug, attached to the end of a bit of string. He twirled it to and fro as he walked. I was now sure that he was mad, and I could scarcely refrain from tears.

We traveled through country where no trace of a human footstep was to be seen.
Legrand led the way. After traveling for more than two hours, with Jupiter cutting
the way through the thick undergrowth with the scythe, we came to the foot of an
enormously tall tree. It was more beautiful than any tree I had ever seen.

Legrand turned to Jupiter and asked him if he thought he could climb the tree.
"Yes," said Jupiter, "I can climb any tree I have ever seen in my life."

Legrand told Jupiter to take the beetle up the tree. When Jupiter had reached the
seventh limb, Legrand told him to go out on the limb as far as he could. "If you see
anything strange, let me know," called Legrand to Jupiter.

By this time I was sure that Legrand was very ill, and I was very anxious to get him
home. But Jupiter called out, "What *is* this on the tree? It's a skull, with a great big
nail in it fastening it to the tree."

Legrand excitedly told Jupiter to let the beetle drop through the left eye of the skull, as far as the string would reach, being careful not to let go of the string.

Soon we saw the beetle hanging quite clear of any branches, glistening in the last rays of the setting sun. Legrand immediately took the scythe, and cleared a circular space just beneath the insect, and then ordered Jupiter to let go of the string and come down from the tree. After a series of measurements, he begged us to start digging as quickly as possible.

There was something in his manner which made me interested, even excited, about what we were doing. We had dug for some time when we were interrupted by the howlings of the dog. He leaped into the hole, and tore at the dirt with his claws. In a few seconds he had uncovered a mass of human bones, forming two complete skeletons. One or two strokes of a spade revealed three or four loose pieces of gold and silver coin. We then unearthed an oblong chest of wood, so heavy we could not lift it, but we could open it. In an instant, a treasure of incalculable value lay gleaming before us. The rays of the lanterns caused a glow and a glare that absolutely dazzled our eyes.

We removed two thirds of the contents of the box, so we could lift the box from the hole. We then hid the articles among the brambles, left the dog to guard them, and took the chest home, arriving there at one o'clock in the morning. We rested until two, and had supper, then left for the hills, armed with three large sacks. We arrived there a little before four, divided the rest of the booty among us, and got back to the hut just as the first streaks of the dawn gleamed from over the treetops in the east.

After a short rest we examined our treasure. There were more than four hundred and fifty thousand dollars in ancient gold coin—French, Spanish, German, and English. There were a hundred and ten large and fine diamonds; eighteen rubies of remarkable brilliancy; three hundred and ten emeralds, all very beautiful; and twenty-one sapphires, with an opal. There were finger and ear rings, heavy gold chains, eighty-three very large and heavy crucifixes, and more things than I can remember. The entire contents of the chest, we estimated, were worth more than a million and a half dollars, but we found later that we had greatly undervalued the treasure.

At last Legrand told us how he had come to discover the treasure. "You remember the night when I handed you the rough sketch I had made of the beetle?" he said. "I became angry with you for suggesting that my drawing resembled a death's-head, for I am considered a good artist. When you handed me the scrap of parchment, I was about to crumple it up and throw it angrily into the fire."

"The scrap of paper, you mean," said I.

"No, it was really parchment, which is usually used for valuable documents. It is more durable than paper. You can imagine my surprise when I saw the figure of a death's-head just where I had made the drawing of the beetle. I took a candle, and began to look at the parchment more carefully. I saw a skull on the other side of the parchment, but I remembered distinctly, positively, that there had been *no* drawing on the parchment when I had made my drawing, because I had looked on both sides of the parchment, in search of the cleanest spot.

"Later I considered the circumstances in which the parchment had come into my possession. While we were trying to catch the beetle, Jupiter was looking about him for a leaf or something to prevent the beetle from biting him, when I found the parchment lying half buried in the sand. Nearby I observed the remnants of the hull of what appeared to have been a ship's longboat. Jupiter picked up the parchment, wrapped the beetle in it, and gave it to me. When I gave the beetle to Lieutenant George, he took it without the parchment, which I must have just put in my pocket. Remember when I was looking for paper to draw the beetle for you? I could find only the parchment. Just as I placed it in your hand, Wolf, the Newfoundland, entered and leaped upon your shoulders. With your left hand you caressed him and kept him off, while your right, holding the parchment, was close to the fire. You must know that chemical preparations exist, by means of which it is possible to write so that the characters shall become visible only when subjected to the action of fire.

"So I kindled a fire, and subjected the parchment to the heat. Soon there appeared the figure of what I at first supposed to be a goat, but I could later see it was meant to be a baby goat—a kid.

"You may have heard of one *Captain* Kidd. You have also heard, of course, of the many rumors about buried treasure in this area. I became convinced that this parchment was an important document, and when I had heated it thoroughly, I found a coded message on the parchment. I assumed, because of the pun on the word Kidd, that it was in English.

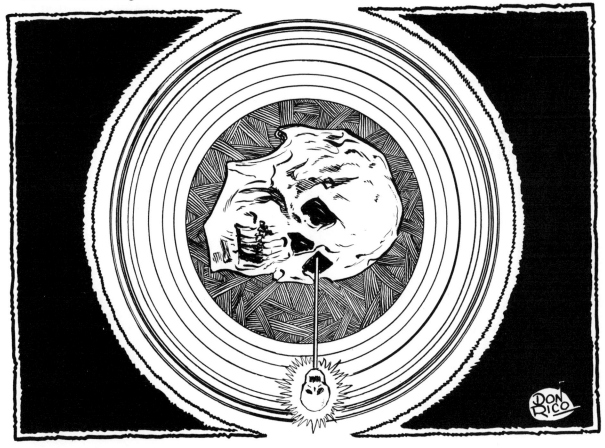

"Now, in English, the letter which most frequently occurs is *e*. Afterwards, the succession runs thus: *a o i d h n r s t u y c f g l m w b k p j v q x z*. Knowing this, and knowing that the most common word in the English language is *the*, I was able to fill in many of the characters in the code. The message finally translated into:

"*A good glass in the Bishop's hostel in the Devil's seat—twenty-one degrees and thirteen minutes—northeast and by north—main branch seventh limb east side—shoot from the left eye of the death's-head—a bee-line from the tree through the shot fifty feet out.*

"The translation was almost as bad as the code, but after having no success in finding Bishop's Hotel (I, of course, had dropped the obsolete word 'hostel'), I thought of the ancient manor house of the Bessop family. A servant at the manor house said she knew of a place called Bessop's Castle, but that it was a high rock.

"When I got there and looked closely at the area, I found a narrow ledge which resembled the hollow-backed chairs used by our ancestors. I thought that this must be the 'Devil's seat' in the riddle, and I knew the 'good glass' could be nothing but a telescope. Degrees and minutes, of course, referred to the directions for the levelling of the glass. 'Main branch, seventh limb, east side' could refer only to the position of the death's-head on the tree, and 'shoot from the left eye of the death's-head' could mean only one thing."

"But why," I asked, "did you insist on letting fall the bug, instead of a bullet, from the skull?"

"Why, I was annoyed by your evident suspicions about my sanity, and so decided to punish you quietly in my own way."

"Now there is only one point which puzzles me. What are we to make of the skeletons found in the hole?"

"That is easy to answer. It is clear that Kidd must have had some help in burying this treasure. Then he must have decided to keep the secret to himself. Perhaps a couple of blows on the head were enough—who shall tell?" ☐

# Mystery at the Library of Congress

*by Ellery Queen*

Ellery responded to a call from Inspector Terence Fineberg with pleasure. Fineberg, in charge of the Central Office, detested amateur detectives, so Ellery knew he must be desperate to have called on him.

"You know Pete Santoria of the Narcotics Squad?" Fineberg said.

Ellery nodded at the stone-jawed Narcotics man.

"We got a line on a new dope ring, Queen," Santoria said. "The junk is coming in from France. New York is the distribution point. We want the boss on the New York end. But all we know so far is that this gang aren't regulars."

"I'll say they're not," Fineberg grumbled. "Who ever heard of a dope smuggler who reads books?"

"Don't tell me we authors are now being blamed for narcotics traffic," Ellery said coldly. "How do books come into this?"

"Using 'em as a code!" Fineberg said. "They've got an information-passing operation going on in Washington. The Federal Bureau of Narcotics is watching two of the D.C. members of the ring."

"One of the two," Santoria continued, "is a colorless little shnook named Balcom, who works for a travel agency. The other—a girl named Norma Shuffing—works at the Library of Congress."

"The Library's being used as a contact rendezvous?" Ellery asked.

"Yes. Balcom passes along information as to when, where, and how a shipment is coming into New York. The contact to whom he has to pass the information is identified for him by the girl. They play it cool—a different contact each time."

"Just what takes place?" Ellery asked intently.

"The girl works at the main desk filling call slips and bringing books onto the floor," Fineberg said. "Balcom always takes the same desk—number 147. When Shuffing spies him, she brings him some books. Balcom looks them over, then looks around the room. And that's all. What we figure happens is, the next day the contact identified through the book titles shows up at the travel agency. Balcom recognizes him and passes him a ticket envelope containing information on the next dope shipment."

"And if you could spot one of these contacts—"

"We could track the dope to the Big Man himself, here in New York."

A contact and shipment, Ellery learned, occurred about every ten days. The Narcotics Squad had set up their first stakeout a month before. At that time Miss Shuffing had brought Balcom three books.

"What were they?"

Inspector Santoria fished a report from a folder. "Steve Allen's *The Funny Men,* Tolstoy's *War and Peace*, and Freud's *Interpretation of Dreams.*"

"Lovely," Ellery murmured. "Freud—Allen—Tolstoy." He seemed disappointed. "It's simple enough. A kindergarten puzzle."

"Sure," Fineberg retorted. "F-A-T. There was a three-hundred pound guy sitting near Balcom."

"The trouble was," Santoria said, "by the time we figured it out, he had gotten his information and taken off. Same thing happened the second time. This time the books were Chekhov's *The Cherry Orchard*, George R. Stewart's *Fire*, and Ben Hecht's *Actor's Blood*."

"*C-S-H*. No sense there," Ellery frowned. "Must be in the titles. No, wait. Cherry-fire-blood. Was there an American Indian nearby? Or someone with red hair?"

"Quick, isn't he, Pete?" Fineberg asked sourly. "Yeah, an old lady with dyed red hair. Only we didn't figure it out until long after she left the library. The third time we missed clean. There was only one book."

"Only *one* book? What was it?"

"Rudyard Kipling's *The Light That Failed.*"

"That's about a man who goes blind. Anybody reading books in Braille?"

"No Braille, no dark glasses, nothing. Only there *was* a dope shipment that week."

Ellery mused. "Do you have a written report of that visit to the library?"

Santoria dug out another folder. Ellery glanced through it. It contained detailed descriptions of suspects and incidents.

"Of course," he said gently. "The old gentleman wearing the clerical collar, trying to light his pipe with a broken lighter. The guard had to remind him that smoking wasn't allowed. 'The Light That Failed'!"

"Let me see that!" Fineberg snatched the folder away. "Pete," he howled, "how the devil did we miss that?"

"We thought for sure there'd be more books, Terence," Santoria stammered. "And the old guy was a preacher—"

"The old guy was a phony! Ellery, how about it? If the next time you could be sitting near Balcom, and maybe spot the contact for us right away—?"

"You couldn't keep me out of this with a court order, Finey," Ellery assured him.

The following Monday Ellery was settled down one desk behind and to the right of number 147 at the Library of Congress. A Federal agent named Hauck was seated where he and Ellery could signal each other. Ellery's desk was loaded with reference books. He was pretending to be an author in search of material, a role he had often played there in earnest.

Norma Shuffing was bringing him an armful of books when a little man, dressed in a mousy business suit, slipped into the seat of Desk 147. Ellery did not need Hauck's signal to identify the newcomer. It was Balcom.

The Shuffing woman passed Desk 147 without a glance.

A quarter of an hour passed.

The reading room began to fill.

Ellery sneaked an inventory of the readers in the vicinity. To Balcom's left sat a buxom woman in a strawberry silk suit. She was raptly reading a volume of industrial reports.

To Balcom's right a large, bald-headed man with wrestler's shoulders was absorbed in a volume on African birds.

Beyond him was a sloppily-dressed Latin whose beard made him look like Fidel Castro. He was making notes from some ancient *National Geographic*s.

Next to the Cuban-looking man was a thin lady intent on the *Congressional Record*.

Also in the neighborhood were a scowling young priest, a businessman with an egg-splattered necktie, and a young woman with a hearing aid.

Suddently the Shuffing woman started up the aisle, lugging a thick, oversize book.

Ellery turned a page. Was this it?

It was!

Miss Shuffing placed the book deftly before Balcom, and walked away. *The Complete Shakespeare.*

Shakespeare. Plays. A playwright? An actor? Nothing about anyone in the room suggested the theater.

Ten minutes later Miss Shuffing laid another book on Desk 147. Ellery craned.

Shaw. Shaw's *Man and Superman.*

A playwright again! But how could you make an instant identification of a playwright—or an actor? *Shakespeare— Shaw. Initials. S. S. SS!* An ex-Nazi Storm trooper? That big bald character who was reading about birds?

Shakespeare, Shaw. English Literature. An Englishman? No; Shaw was Irish.

Ellery shook his head. What the devil was the girl trying to convey to Balcom?

A third book was coming. The Shuffing girl placed it on Desk 147. Ellery could barely contain himself. He blessed his sharp eyesight.

*Personal Memoirs of U.S. Grant.*

Blam went his theories! Two playwrights, one military man. SS, now G. An Englishman, an Irishman, and an American. What did it all add up to?

Shakespeare . . . Shaw . . . General Grant . . .

*Balcom had it!*

He was looking around casually now, as if one glimpse was all he needed.

Ellery struggled with panic. Any moment now Balcom's contact might get up and leave, knowing Balcom had spotted him. People were constantly coming and going. It would be impossible to identify the right one without the clue conveyed by the books. Ellery could already hear Santoria's horse laugh.

And then—O blessed!—he had it, too. Ellery rose. He strolled up the aisle past Agent Hauck, and out into the Washington sunshine. Inspector Santoria and a second Federal man were in an unmarked car. Ellery slipped into the rear seat.

Agent Hauck came out two minutes later. "Get set for the tail," Ellery said. "The contact is sitting two seats to Balcom's right. The sloppy Cuban guy."

"Afternoon, Finey," Ellery said on Friday of that week.

"Sit down, my boy," Inspector Terence Fineberg said cordially. "You're ace-high around here. Thought you'd like to know Pete Santoria collared Big Stuff two hours ago, in the act of taking possession of a shipment of narcotics. The Narcotics Squad is out right now picking up Balcom and the girl. By the way, that Havana number was never closer to Cuba than an El Stinko cigar. He's a poolroom punk from Brooklyn name of Harry Hummelmayer. Meanwhile, I've been going nuts trying to figure out a connection between Shakespeare, Shaw, and Grant."

"With Hummelmayer looking like Fidel Castro?" Ellery reached over the desk and waggled Inspector Fineberg's knotty chin. "Beards, Finey, they all had beards!"  □

# THE NECKLACE

## by Guy de Maupassant

She was a pretty, charming young lady, born, as if through an error of fate, into a family of office workers. The sight of her husband, a petty clerk in the Board of Education, awakened in her sad regrets and desperate dreams. When at dinner he would say, "Oh! The good potpie! I know nothing better than that—" she would think of elegant banquets, shining silver, exquisite food served on marvelous china.

She suffered from the poverty of her life. She had neither dresses nor jewelry— nothing. And yet she felt that she was made for these things. She had a rich friend, Madame Forestier, whom she did not like to visit. She suffered so much afterward, weeping from despair and disappointment.

One evening her husband came home elated, carrying a large envelope. "Here is something for you!" he said.

She quickly tore open the envelope and drew out a printed card on which she read:

> *"The Minister of Education and Madame Georges Ramponneau ask the honor of Monsieur and Madame Loisel's company Monday evening, January 18, at the Minister's residence."*

Madame Loisel threw the invitation spitefully upon the table. "What would I want with that?" she murmured.

"But, my dear, I thought it would make you happy. You never go out, and this is a fine occasion—" He was stupefied at the sight of his wife weeping. "What is the matter?" he stammered.

"Nothing," she responded, wiping her moist cheeks. "Only I have nothing to wear to such an affair. Give your card to someone whose wife is better fitted out than I."

He was grieved, but answered, "Let us see, Matilda. How much would a suitable costume cost, something very simple?"

She thought for some seconds, wondering what she could ask without being immediately refused. "I cannot tell exactly," she said in a hesitating voice, "but I think that four hundred francs would do."

Her husband had saved just this sum to buy a gun for going hunting with his friends. Nevertheless he answered, "Very well. I will give you four hundred francs. But try to have a pretty dress."

The day of the ball approached, and Madame Loisel's dress was ready. Nevertheless she seemed sad, disturbed, anxious. "What is the matter?" her husband asked her.

"I have no jewelry, nothing to adorn myself with," she replied. "I would rather not go to this party."

"You can wear flowers," he suggested. "At this season roses look very fashionable."

"No," she replied. "There is nothing more humiliating than to appear shabby in the midst of rich women."

Then her husband cried out, "How stupid we are! Ask your friend Madame Forestier to lend you some jewels. You know her well enough."

She uttered a cry of joy. "It is true!" she said. "I had not thought of that."

The next day she went to her friend's house and told her of her distress. Madame Forestier brought out a large jewel case. "Choose, my dear," she said.

She tried the jewels before a mirror, but could not decide which to take. Then she discovered a superb diamond necklace. Her heart beat fast and her hands trembled as she lifted it. "Could you lend me this?" she asked. "Only this?"

"Why, yes, certainly."

She fell upon the neck of her friend and embraced her with passion.

At the ball Madame Loisel was a great success. She was the prettiest of all, elegant, smiling, joyful. All the government officials wished to dance with her. Even the Minister of Education paid her some attention. She passed the evening in a cloud of happiness.

She went home toward four o'clock in the morning. In the street she and her husband could find no carriage. They walked along the Seine, hopeless and shivering. Finally they found one of those old coupés that one sees in Paris after nightfall, as if they were ashamed of their shabbiness by day.

It took them to their door, and they went wearily up to their apartment. It was all over for her. She removed her cloak before the mirror, for a final view of herself in her glory. Suddenly she cried out.

"I have—I have—I no longer have the necklace!"

Her husband, already half undressed, arose in dismay. "What? How is that? It is not possible."

And they looked in the folds of the dress, in the pockets of her cloak, everywhere. They could not find it.

He asked, "You are sure you still had it when we left the house?"

"Yes, I felt it as we came out."

"But if you had lost it in the street, we would have heard it fall. It must be in the cab."

"Yes. It is probable. Did you notice the number?"

"No."

They looked at each other, utterly cast down. Finally Loisel dressed himself again. "I am going to see if I can find it," he said.

And he went. She remained in her evening gown, stretched on a chair, not having the strength to go to bed.

Toward seven o'clock her husband returned. He had found nothing.

He went to the police and to the cab offices. He put an advertisement in the papers, offering a reward.

At the end of a week they had lost all hope. And Loisel, looking older by five years, declared, "We must replace the necklace."

They went from jeweler to jeweler seeking a necklace like the other one. In the shop of the Palais-Royal they found one, priced at thirty-six thousand francs.

Loisel's father had left him eighteen thousand francs. He borrowed the rest. He risked his signature, not knowing whether he could make it good or not. After three days, full of horror of what the future now held in store for him, he presented the jeweler with thirty-six thousand francs.

When Madame Loisel returned the necklace, Madame Forestier said to her in an icy tone, "You should have returned it sooner, for I might have needed it."

Madame Loisel now knew the horrible life of real poverty. She did her part, however, completely and heroically. It was necessary to pay this frightful debt. She would pay it. They sent away the maid. They moved to a poorer part of town.

She learned the heavy cares of a household. She broke her tender nails on greasy pans and the bottoms of stewpots. She took down the garbage to the street every morning and brought up the water. And, dressed like a low-class woman, she went to the market with her basket on her arm, haggling to the last cent.

Her husband worked evenings, putting the books of merchants in order, and nights he did copying at five cents a page.

And this life lasted ten years.

At the end of ten years they had repaid all, with interest.

Madame Loisel seemed old now. She had become the crude woman of a poor household. But sometimes, seated before the window, she would remember that ball where she was so beautiful and so flattered.

How would it have been if she had not lost that necklace! Who knows? How strange is life, and how full of changes. How small a thing will ruin or save one!

One Sunday, as she was taking a walk to forget the cares of the week, she saw a woman walking with a child. It was Madame Forestier, still looking young and pretty. Madame Loisel was moved. Should she speak to her? Yes, why not? Now that she had paid, she would tell all.

She approached her. "Good morning, Jeanne."

Her friend was astonished to be so familiarly addressed by such a common person. "But, Madame—I do not know—you must be mistaken—"

"No, I am Matilda Loisel."

"Oh! My poor Matilda!" her friend cried out. "How you have changed—"

"Yes, I have had some hard days since I saw you—and all because of you."

"Because of me? How is that?"

"You recall the diamond necklace that you loaned me?"

"Yes, very well."

"Well, I lost it."

"How can that be? You returned it to me!"

"I returned to you another exactly like it. And it has taken us ten years to pay for it. You understand that it was not easy for us who have nothing. But it is finished, and I am decently content."

Madame Forestier held out her hand. "Oh! My poor Matilda!" she said. "But my diamonds were false! They were not worth more than five hundred francs!"    □

# THE THREE STRANGERS

### by *Thomas Hardy*

Among the few features of agricultural England which change but little through the centuries are the high and grassy narrow valleys. If there is any sign of human occupation here, it is usually in the form of the solitary cottage of some shepherd.

Fifty years ago such a lonely cottage stood in such a place, and may still be there. In spite of its loneliness, it was but five miles from a town. *Higher Crowstairs*, as the house was called, was located at the crossing of two footpaths.

The night of March 28, 1823, the shepherd who lived there was entertaining a large party for the christening of his second girl. The guests had arrived before the rain began to fall, and they were all now in the living room of the small dwelling. And it was as cozy and comfortable a dwelling as could be wished for in such stormy weather. New candles were scattered about the room and a fire blazed in the fireplace.

Shepherd Fennel had married well, his wife being frugal and smart. A sit-still party had its advantages, she knew, but it led the men to so much drinking that they would sometimes drink the house dry. A dancing party would cut down on the drinking, but would increase appetites. For this party, therefore, she had decided to mix short dances with short periods of talk and singing.

While these cheerful events were taking place within Fennel's pastoral dwelling, a human figure came up the solitary hill of *Higher Crowstairs* from the direction of the distant town. The sad light of the moon revealed the man to be about forty years of age. He appeared tall, but this was probably because he was so gaunt.

74

He seemed to travel carefully, as if he were not used to the area. By the time he arrived at the shepherd's cottage, the rain was coming down even harder than before. He stood outside in the shelter of a pigpen, and listened to the music within the cottage. When the music finally stopped, he emerged from the shed and walked up the path to the house door. He lifted his hand to knock, but stopped with his eye upon the panel. In his indecision he turned and looked at the scene around. Not a soul was anywhere to be seen. The absence of any sign of life seemed to clinch his intentions, and he knocked at the door.

"Walk in!" said the shepherd promptly.

The latch clicked upward, and out of the night our traveler appeared. The light showed that the stranger was dark and good-looking. His eyes were large and moved with a flash rather than a glance around the room. In a rich deep voice, he said, "The rain is so heavy, friends, that I ask to come in and rest awhile."

"To be sure, stranger," said the shepherd. "And, you are lucky in choosing your time, for we are having a party for a glad cause."

"And what may be this glad cause?" asked the stranger.

"A birth and a christening," said the shepherd.

Being invited to have a drink of mead, he accepted, and sat in the chimney corner, stretching out his legs and his arms with the manner of a person quite at home.

"Yes, my boots are a bit cracked," he said, seeing that the eyes of the shepherd's wife fell upon his boots. "I have had some rough times lately. I have been forced to pick up what I can get in the way of wearing."

Meanwhile the rest of the guests had been talking with the band about a tune for the next dance. The matter being settled, they were about to stand up when there was another knock at the door.

At the sound of this, the man in the chimney corner started to stir the fire as if doing it well were the one aim of his life. A second time the shepherd said, "Walk in!" In a moment another stranger stood at the door.

This man was quite different from the first. He was several years older. His hair was slightly frosty, his eyebrows full, and his whiskers cut back from his cheeks. His face was rather full and flabby. Under his overcoat, he wore a suit of cinder gray color. "I must ask for a few minutes' shelter, friends, or I shall be wetted to my skin before I get to Casterbridge."

"Make yourself at home, master," said the shepherd.

The second stranger sat down at the table, which had been pushed closely into the chimney corner, to give room to the dancers; thus the two strangers were brought into close companionship. The first stranger handed his neighbor the mug from which he had been drinking. The other man raised the mug to his lips, and drank on, and on, and on.

"I knew it!" said the second stranger. "When I walked through your garden and saw the hives in a row, I said to myself, 'Where there's bees there's honey, and where there's honey, there's mead.' This mead is delicious!" Soon the mug needed

refilling, and the frugal wife of the shepherd brought him a smaller glass.

The conversation soon turned to the occupations of the strangers. The man in the chimney corner said, "I repair wheels," but the second stranger began to speak in riddles about his trade. To the music, he sang:

> *"My tools are but common ones,*
> *Simple shepherds all—*
> *My tools are no sight to see:*
> *A little string, and a post from which to swing,*
> *Are tools enough for me!"*

"Oh, he's the—" whispered the people in the background. "He's come to do it. It's to be at Casterbridge jail tomorrow—the man for sheep stealing—the poor clockmaker we heard of, who had no work to do—Timothy Summers, whose family was starving—"

The stranger in cinder gray took no notice of the whispers, but drank some more, clinking glasses with his friend in the chimney corner, the only one who seemed to be jolly.

Then, for the third time, there was a knock upon the door. This time the knock was faint and hesitating. "Walk in!" said the shepherd.

The door was gently opened, and a third stranger stood upon the mat. He was a short, small person, of fair complexion, and dressed in a decent overcoat.

"Can you tell me the way to—" he began, just as the stranger in cinder gray began singing another verse:—

*"Tomorrow is my working day,*
*Simple shepherds all—*
*Tomorrow is a working day for me:*
*For the farmer's sheep is slain, and the lad who did it taken,*
*And on his soul God have mercy!"*

All this time the third stranger had been standing in the doorway. The guests noticed to their surprise that he stood before them the picture of terror—his knees trembling, his hand shaking violently, and his eyes fixed on the merry officer of justice in the middle of the room. A moment more and he had turned, closed the door, and fled.

"Who might that have been?" said the shepherd.

The guests were silent, so that nothing could be heard but the patter of the rain and the steady puffing of the man in the corner, who was smoking a long clay pipe.

The stillness was suddenly broken by the distant sound of a gun.

"What does that mean?" asked several of the guests.

"A prisoner escaped from the jail—that's what it means."

"I wonder if it is *my* man?" said the man in cinder gray.

"Surely it is!" said the shepherd. "And surely we've seen him. The man who looked in at the door just now, and shook like a leaf when he saw you and heard your song!"

"True—his teeth chattered, and his heart seemed to sink, and he ran as if he'd been shot at," slowly said the man in the chimney corner.

The evidence was so convincing that the men, aroused by the hangman, prepared to give chase. The child who had been christened began to cry in the room overhead, so that the women jumped up one by one to go upstairs. Thus in two or three minutes the room was deserted.

But it was not for long. Hardly had the sound of footsteps died away when the two strangers returned to take another piece of cake. Both said that they thought the shepherds did not need any more help in catching the criminal. After their conversation, they shook hands heartily at the door, and wishing each other well, they went in opposite directions.

Meantime, the company of pursuers had come near a lonely tree. Standing a little to one side of the trunk was the man they were in search of. His fear seemed to be completely gone.

"You must come and be our prisoner at once! We arrest you for not being in Casterbridge jail to be hung tomorrow morning."

On hearing the charge, the man seemed enlightened, and saying not another word, resigned himself with courtesy to the search party. They surrounded him on all sides, and marched him back toward the shepherd's cottage.

On entering the cottage, they found two officers from Casterbridge jail.

"Who is this?" said one of the officials.

"The man you are looking for."

"Certainly not," said the jail officer. "He is not the one. The condemned man's quite a different character from this one; a gaunt fellow, with dark hair and eyes, rather good-looking, and with a musical deep voice."

"Why, it was the man in the chimney corner!"

The prisoner now spoke for the first time. "The time is come when I may as well speak. I have done nothing. My crime is that the condemned man is my brother. Early this afternoon I left home to walk to Casterbridge jail to bid him farewell. I was lost, and stopped here to ask the way. When I opened the door I saw before me the very man, my brother, that I thought to see in the condemned cell at Casterbridge. He was in the chimney corner. Close to him was the executioner who'd come to take his life, singing a song about it and not knowing that it was his victim who was close by, joining in to save appearances. My brother looked a glance of agony at me, and I knew he meant, 'Don't reveal what you see. My life depends on it.' I was so terror-struck that I could hardly stand, and, not knowing what I did, I turned and hurried away."

"Do you know where your brother is now?"

"I do not. I have not seen him since I closed this door."

"Where can he go? What is his occupation?"

"He's a watch and clockmaker, sir."

"He said he was a repairer of wheels, the wicked rogue."

"The wheels of clocks and watches he meant, no doubt," said Shepherd Fennel.

So the third stranger was released, and the next day, the search for the clever sheep stealer continued. But the intended punishment was too harsh for the crime, and most of the people in the district were on the side of the fugitive. Also, his marvelous coolness and daring in being friendly with the hangman had won everyone's admiration. So it may be questioned if all those who were so busy searching the woods and fields were quite so thorough when it came to searching their own haylofts. And the days and weeks passed without anyone turning in the sheep stealer.

At any rate, the gentleman in cinder gray never did his morning's work in Caster-bridge, nor did he meet anywhere the pleasant stranger with whom he had passed an hour of relaxation in the lonely house in the valley.

The grass has long been green on the graves of Shepherd Fennel and his frugal wife. Most of the guests at the christening party have followed their entertainers to the tomb. The baby in whose honor they all had met is an old woman. But the story of the three strangers is a story as well known as ever in the country about *Higher Crowstairs.* □

# DR. JEKYLL AND MR. HYDE

### by Robert Louis Stevenson

Mr. Utterson the lawyer was fond of his Sunday afternoon walks with his young cousin, Richard Enfield. It happened one Sunday that their way led them down a side street in a busy quarter of London. The brightness of this block was broken by one sinister-looking building with a courtyard beyond, and a door which opened onto the street.

"That door reminds me of a very odd story," Mr. Enfield remarked.

"Indeed?" said Mr. Utterson.

"I was walking home very late one night," said Mr. Enfield, "when I saw a man knock down a little girl. Well, of course, I collared the gentleman. He didn't resist, but he gave me a look that made my blood run cold! The child was rather more frightened than hurt, but I told this loathesome creature that if he didn't come up with a hundred pounds for her family, I would make his name stink all over London. Now, when he went to get the money, he led me to this very door! He came out with a check signed with a very respected name, which I will not mention. Naturally, I was sure it was a forgery. 'Set your mind at rest,' this evil little man sneered. 'When the bank opens I'll go with you and cash it myself.' Well, sir, the check proved to be perfectly genuine."

"Enfield," said the lawyer, after a long pause, "this sounds like a bad business."

"Indeed, sir. An honest man paying through the nose for a youthful indiscretion. That's what I make of it."

"There's one thing I want to ask," said Mr. Utterson. "Could you tell me the name of this monster?"

"Well," said Mr. Enfield, "I don't suppose it will compromise anyone. The man's name was Hyde. Edward Hyde."

This was as the lawyer had feared. That door was in fact the rear entrance to the laboratory of his friend, Dr. Henry Jekyll. And, months before, Dr. Jekyll had changed his will, providing that in the event of his "death or disappearance," all of his considerable wealth should pass to one Edward Hyde.

Mr. Utterson now was certain that Jekyll was being blackmailed by Hyde. From that day Mr. Utterson began to haunt the side street. "If he shall be Mr. Hyde," he thought, "I shall be Mr. Seek."

Late one evening his patience was rewarded. A small, plainly dressed man appeared and headed straight for the door, drawing a key from his pocket.

Mr. Utterson stepped forward and touched him on the shoulder. "Mr. Hyde, I think?"

The man shrank back with a sharp breath. "That is my name," he hissed. "What do you want?"

Mr. Hyde seemed deformed, without any recognizable deformity. But this appearance alone could not explain the fear and disgust he raised in Mr. Utterson.

The lawyer's concern for his friend, Dr. Jekyll, overcame his discomfort.

"I see you are going in," said the lawyer. "I am an old friend of Dr. Jekyll's, and I thought you might admit me."

"Dr. Jekyll is not at home," replied Mr. Hyde. "How did you know me?"

"By description. We have common friends."

"Common friends?" echoed Mr. Hyde. "Who are they?"

"Jekyll, for instance."

"Liar! He never told you!" said Hyde, and in one quick movement he unlocked the door and disappeared into the house.

The lawyer stood there for a moment, shaken. "God help poor Jekyll," he thought. "No doubt there is some dark secret in his past which Hyde is threatening to expose. That man has the Devil's look upon his face!"

Two weeks later, by good fortune, the doctor invited several old friends to dinner. Dr. Jekyll sat quietly by the fire. A large, well-made man of fifty, he gave no sign that his life was in any way troubled. As he often did on these occasions, Utterson remained behind after the other guests had gone.

"I have been wanting to speak to you, Jekyll," the lawyer began. "It's about that will of yours. I've been learning something about young Hyde."

At once the doctor's handsome face grew pale. "I do not care to hear more," he said. "This is a matter I thought we had agreed to drop."

"But what I heard was abominable," said Utterson.

"It can make no difference. You do not understand," returned the doctor. "The situation is a strange one, Utterson, and cannot be mended by talking."

"Jekyll," said Utterson, "you know I can be trusted. Whatever trouble you may be in, I want to help you."

"My dear Utterson," said the doctor, "this is very good of you, but it isn't as bad as you fancy. The moment I choose, I can be rid of Mr. Hyde. I give you my hand on that. I'm sure you'll understand, but this is a private matter and I beg of you to let it sleep."

Utterson gazed into the fire. "Well," he said, heaving a sigh, "I have no doubt that you are perfectly right."

It was nearly a year later, in October, 1883, that London was shocked by the murder of Sir Danvers Carew. A housemaid happened to be looking out of a window and had witnessed the crime. The distinguished-looking gentleman had stopped to ask directions of another man. The second man had burst out angrily, brandishing a heavy cane and carrying on like a madman. In the gaslight the maid recognized him as a Mr. Hyde, who had once called upon her employer. In the next moment he clubbed the old gentleman to the ground. Then, like an ape, he was trampling his victim and raining blows upon him.

The police found the broken half of the murderer's cane beside the body. In the victim's pocket was a letter addressed to Mr. Utterson. The lawyer was sent for.

"Good God!" exclaimed the policeman. "Sir Danvers Carew! Is this possible?" He briefly related what the maid had seen, and showed Utterson the broken stick.

The lawyer had already jumped at the name of Hyde. But when the stick was laid before him, there was no longer any doubt. It was one he had himself presented many years before to Henry Jekyll.

It was late afternoon when Mr. Utterson arrived at Dr. Jekyll's house. He was let in by Poole, the elderly butler, who showed him across the yard to the laboratory. It was the first time he had ever been in that part of his friend's quarters. There was a strangeness about the place, with its tables laden with chemical apparatus. Dr. Jekyll sat near a fire, looking deadly sick.

"You have heard the news?" said Mr. Utterson.

The doctor shuddered. "They were crying it in the square," he said.

"One word," said the lawyer. "Carew was my client, but so are you. I would like to be able to keep your name out of a trial. You have not been so mad as to hide this fellow, have you?"

"Utterson, I swear that I am done with him," cried the doctor. "He will never again be heard from."

"I hope you are right," said the lawyer. "He might just as easily have murdered you! You have had a fine escape!"

"I have had more than that," returned the doctor. "I have had a lesson. Oh God, Utterson, what a lesson I have had!" He covered his face with his hands.

Time went on. A reward was offered, but Mr. Hyde had disappeared. In the meantime, Dr. Jekyll seemed healthy and at peace with himself.

Then on the 12th of January, Mr. Utterson was denied entrance to Jekyll's house. "The doctor is not well," Poole said, "and will see no one." The following day Utterson was again refused. As soon as he got home, the lawyer sat down and wrote to Jekyll, asking an explanation.

"I mean from now on to live a life of extreme seclusion," Jekyll wrote in answer. "You must not doubt my friendship, but you must allow me to go along my own dark way. . . ."

Then one evening Utterson received a visit from Poole. "What is wrong?" he asked, seeing the old servant's face. "Is the doctor ill?"

"Mr. Utterson," said the man, "I have never been so frightened. He's shut himself up in his laboratory, and—well, I'm afraid sir. I think there has been foul play. I ought to know the voice of the man I've served for twenty years. It's somebody else in there!"

"This is a strange tale, Poole," said the lawyer. "Suppose somebody had—well, murdered Dr. Jekyll. Why would he stay? Why hasn't he fled?"

"All I can tell you," said Poole, "is that we've seen nothing of the master for eight days. We leave his meals by the door. He throws notes on the stair, two or three times a day, ordering us to fetch some sort of medicine. I've been to every wholesale chemist's in London. But each time there was another note telling me that the stuff was not pure, and another order to a different company. At times I hear him pacing, or wailing like a lost soul."

Mr. Utterson rose and got his hat and overcoat.

It was a wild, cold night. The wind seemed to have swept the streets bare, for Mr. Utterson thought he had never seen London so deserted.

The hall of Jekyll's house was brightly lit. Around the fire the servants stood huddled like a flock of sheep.

"They're all afraid," Poole murmured.

"With good reason, I am sure," said Mr. Utterson. "Call your footman."

"Bradshaw!" said Poole, and a young man, very white and nervous, stepped forward.

"Pull yourself together, Bradshaw," said the lawyer. "We are going to force our way into the laboratory, if necessary. I want you to bring an axe." Taking a poker under his arm, Utterson followed Poole across the yard to the laboratory.

"Jekyll," called Utterson, "I demand to see you."

"Utterson," cried a voice from within, "for God's sake, have mercy!"

"Ah, that's not Jekyll's voice—it's Hyde's!" cried Utterson. "Down with the door!" Bradshaw swung his axe; the door leaped against the lock and hinges. A screech of animal terror rang from the laboratory. At the fifth blow of the axe, the door fell inward.

The besiegers peered in. On the floor lay the body of Edward Hyde. He was dressed in clothes far too large for him—Jekyll's clothes. By the crushed capsule in his hand, Utterson knew that he was looking on the body of a suicide.

"We have come too late," he said, "whether to save or punish. It only remains for us to find your master."

They searched the laboratory, but could find no trace of Henry Jekyll, dead or alive. Suddenly Utterson noticed a sheet of paper on the desk. It was in the doctor's hand and dated at the top. "Poole!" the lawyer cried. "He was alive and here today! He must still be alive; he must have fled! But why? And how?" He read as follows:

*"My dear Utterson,—When this shall fall into your hands, I shall have disappeared. Read the contents of the sealed packet which you will find in this desk, and all will be explained.*

*"Your unworthy and unhappy friend, "Henry Jekyll"*

Quickly Poole located the packet. Utterson broke the seals and began to read the narrative in which the mystery was now to be explained.

## HENRY JEKYLL'S FULL STATEMENT OF THE CASE

*I was born to a large fortune, and endowed besides with talent and ability. As public reputation has always been of the greatest importance to me, I learned in my youth to conceal my pleasures and low passions. Many men flaunt such irregularities; I hid them with a deep sense of shame.*

As a result the twin urges toward good and evil, which all men possess, were in myself even more deeply divided. I came to realize that man is not truly one, but two. If each, I thought, could be housed in separate identities, there need be no shame. The evil could go his own way, unrestrained by guilt. The good would need no longer fear disgrace.

And so I directed my research toward the separation of these two opposite identities. There is no need to describe in detail my experiments. They came to an end late one accursed night. I had obtained the last of the chemicals I needed. I mixed them in a glass, watched them boil and smoke together, and with a strong glow of courage, drank them down.

The most horrible, grinding pains followed. But they quickly subsided. There was something incredibly sweet in my sensations. My body felt younger and lighter. I was aware of a new, reckless freedom of the soul. From the first breath I knew I was ten times more wicked. I was a slave to my original evil. This thought acted on me like wine. I was delighted. I looked into a mirror, and saw for the first time the face of Edward Hyde.

From that night I had two characters and two identities. One was entirely evil; the other was the same old Henry Jekyll. I could change myself at will from one to the other. As Hyde I could do what I pleased, without fearing the consequences. I needed only to slip into the laboratory, drink the potion, and re-appear as Jekyll.

The pleasures I had sought had been, at worst, undignified. But in the hands of Edward Hyde, they soon became monstrous. Though other men have within them a mixture of good and evil, Hyde was purely evil. But the situation was apart from ordinary laws, and this relaxed Jekyll's conscience. It was Hyde alone that was guilty. As Jekyll, I thought I stood beyond the reach of fate.

One morning, about two months before the murder of Sir Danvers, I awoke with odd sensations. I was still only half awake when I happened to gaze upon my hand. I must have stared at it for half a minute before I realized what I was seeing. I had gone to bed as Henry Jekyll; I had awakened as Edward Hyde!

The danger was clear. I was losing hold of my original and better self. If this went on much longer, the character of Hyde would become permanently mine.

I made my choice. I would remain Dr. Jekyll. But as time passed I began to be tortured with longing to become the evil Hyde once again. At last, in an hour of weakness, I again transformed myself.

My devil had long been caged; he came out roaring. I was aware, even as I drank the potion, of a more furious urge toward evil. The spirit of hell awoke in me.

*It was in this spirit that I murdered Carew.*

*Once I had returned to my better form, I was filled with remorse. There was no question this time; Edward Hyde must disappear forever. But the balance of my soul had been tipped. The dark side of my nature, so recently chained down, began to growl for freedom. I was sitting one afternoon in Regent's Park, the animal within me licking the chops of memory. Suddenly a deadly shuddering came over me. Even as it passed I was aware that I was once more Edward Hyde—a hunted murderer.*

*It was by a miracle that he—I cannot say I—was able to steal back to the laboratory. Once I was myself again, I realized that a change had come over me. It was no longer the fear of the gallows that racked me, but the horror of being Hyde. Yet I was once more at home, close to my drugs. Gratitude for my escape was as strong within me as the brightness of hope.*

*Stepping across the court after breakfast, I was once again seized with the feelings of change. Again the passions of Hyde raged within me. This time it took a double dose to restore Dr. Jekyll. And six hours later I was Hyde again!*

Since that day it has only been through a great effort of will, and for ever-shorter periods of time, that I have been able to wear the face of Jekyll. At any hour I may suddenly change. If I fall asleep, it is always as Hyde that I awaken. I write this document under the influence of the last of the drugs. If Hyde should find it before it is completed, he will tear it in pieces. What will be his end? The gallows? Suicide? Whatever becomes of Hyde, this is the true hour of my death. What is to follow concerns another than myself. Here, then, as I lay down the pen, I bring the life of that unhappy Henry Jekyll to an end.  □